About Paying it Fo

I am always so proud each year to share the incredible progress being made by the Stefanie Spielman Fund for Breast Cancer Research at The Ohio State University Comprehensive Cancer Center – Arthur G. James Cancer Hospital and Richard J. Solove Research Institute (OSUCCC – James). The researchers and clinicians work tirelessly every day to develop new and innovative treatment options for patients through research, drug development, and clinical trials. This would not be possible without the incredible support of our Columbus community and from friends across the country that share my family's commitment to finding a cure.

As the great OSU Football Coach Woody Hayes always encouraged, we owe it to ourselves and to others to pay it forward. My wife, Stefanie, believed passionately that her disease was given to her so that she could help others. I believe she paid it forward every day from the moment she was diagnosed. We are grateful that as of 2014, more than $15 million dollars has been raised to support the Spielman Fund thanks to supporters, like you, who believe in paying it forward. Through that generosity, the OSUCCC – James has the ability to reach new heights with breast cancer research, patient care, and training for our future cancer experts.

Thank you for supporting the cause through the purchase of this book.

God Bless,
Chris Spielman

www.mascotbooks.com

The Day I Met Woody

©2014 Roy C. Roychoudhury. All Rights Reserved. No part of this publication may be reproduced, stored in a retrieval system or transmitted in any form by any means electronic, mechanical, or photocopying, recording or otherwise without the permission of the author.

For more information, please contact:
Mascot Books
560 Herndon Parkway #120
Herndon, VA 20170
info@mascotbooks.com

CPSIA Code: PRT1014A
ISBN-13: 9781620864678

Trademarks are Officially licensed by The Ohio State University.

Printed in the United States

-The Day I Met-
WOODY

by **Roy C. Roychoudhury**

illustrated by Lydia Ferron

THIS BOOK IS DEDICATED TO MY WIFE, ANYA, AND MY DAUGHTERS, EMERSON ELIZABETH AND MAEVE ANNE PARKER, AND MY BROTHER, RAJ. THANK YOU SO MUCH FOR YOUR NEVER-ENDING SUPPORT AND LOVE. WITH IT, SO MANY GREAT THINGS ARE POSSIBLE. MAY I BE ABLE TO CONTINUE TO PAY IT FORWARD FOR ALL OF MY BLESSINGS. GO BUCKS!

Foreword by Cornelius Green

Woody Hayes cared about people. I had the good fortune of experiencing this firsthand by playing football for Coach Hayes at The Ohio State University during four of the most formative years of my life. Woody taught me so much more than how to be a better football player. Coach Hayes taught me to be a leader. Woody taught me that true achievement and success come only from "Paying Forward" all of your gifts from those parents, coaches, and teachers that touched your life. Roy Roychoudhury's *The Day I Met Woody* is a wonderful testament to Coach Hayes, and the life lessons he taught those who crossed his path. Woody's love for reading, as well as his passion for the works of Ralph Waldo Emerson, comes across strongly in this book. Roy's personal story of meeting Woody, as depicted in this book, fondly reminds me of the many lives I personally saw Coach Hayes forever touch through random encounters such as these. I can remember the hundreds of children's hospital rooms Woody would personally visit or make sure that his players (like me) would drop by with words of encouragement. Woody Hayes cared about people no matter their race, religion, or culture. If you want to share your love for Ohio State and passion about Woody Hayes, I cannot think of a better way than reading this book with those you love. I hope you enjoy sharing *The Day I Met Woody* with your kids and grandkids as much as I have with those closest to me.

Go Bucks and Pay it Forward today!

Cornelius Green
OSU MVP
Rose Bowl MVP
OSU Team Captain
OSU Hall of Fame

Growing up in Ohio in the 1970s meant that you knew about Woody Hayes. I watched my dad, my mom, my brothers, and my sister watch Woody coach the Buckeyes every fall.

Little did I know, that one day, I would actually meet Woody and he would change my life forever.

When I was little, the more
I would see or read about
Woody and the Buckeyes, the
more I thought I understood.

I KNEW WOODY LOVED HIS PLAYERS.

I KNEW WOODY LOVED OHIO STATE.

I KNEW WOODY LOVED TO READ.

I KNEW WOODY LOVED TO WORK HARD.

One day, I was invited to a football camp at Ohio State with some of my friends from school. It was going to be a fun day where we would learn how to do the things that we saw the Buckeyes do during games. We would also learn what the Buckeyes do in practice.

The night before, I was so excited that I could not wait for the next morning to arrive.

As soon as I opened my eyes, I woke up and I didn't have to wait for Mama to tell me what to do. I had to get to the football camp as soon as possible. I quickly brushed my teeth. I fed the dog **SUPER FAST**. I got dressed in record time. I never moved so quickly before in my life.

Somehow, my mom and dad could tell that I was looking forward to my big day. I was waiting for my friend and his dad to pick me up, and when I saw the car pull in, it became real. We were actually going to Ohio State!

I found out in the car that what we were going to was actually called a "football clinic." That seemed fun. It was not going to be at the stadium, but it was going to be at The Ohio State University Golf Course.

Would we play golf, too? I thought. I am going to have so much fun with my friends!

When we finally arrived, we all got out of the car and we saw all sorts of people already there. We listened well and followed all the directions and finally, the football clinic began.

I even saw some real Buckeye football players ready to teach us. Real players like Chris Spielman, Cris Carter, and Sonny Gordon were all there. I couldn't believe the players I watched so many times were right here waiting to teach me how to play!

Then it happened… BLUGHGHGHGHG, I heard my stomach talking to me. I pretended not to hear it but then my tummy spoke again, a bit louder, BLUGHGHGHGH. This time my stomach gave me a nice little punch from the inside to make sure I felt it. I felt like my tummy was in knots!

All my friends were running around, having a great time, and my tummy was in knots. I ran up to Sonny Gordon, who was helping run the clinic, and told him that my stomach hurt. He told me to sit out for a few minutes and rest.

I could not believe it. *I never get sick. I never get sick on days so important. There were my friends having a great time. Why did this happen to me?*

I was sitting under a tree and my stomach kept talking to me over and over again, BLUGHGHGHGH!

Why, tummy? Why are you doing this to me? I was so sad that I couldn't feel anything except for how upset I was that I could not play.

All of a sudden, I heard a golf cart driving over a hill. All I could see was an older man in one seat and a younger man driving. The old man pointed at me! Then they started driving towards me! Could this day get any worse?

My tummy must be playing tricks on me, I thought, as the golf cart got closer. *That old man looks like Woody.*

The golf cart pulled up and I could not believe it. It was Woody!

Woody paused, but his driver looked ready to move on. "What's your name?" asked Woody.

I froze again. *Was my name* BLUGHGHGHGH? I thought before I answered, "It's Roy, Coach." I remembered that my dad said to always call a coach, "Coach."

Woody looked at me from the top of my head all the way to my shoes. Then he spoke, "I know you are disappointed that you can't be out there with your friends. The important thing to remember is to always get better, **EVERY DAY**. So when you feel better, you can work harder and make sure that the next day, you can do a little bit more than you did today."

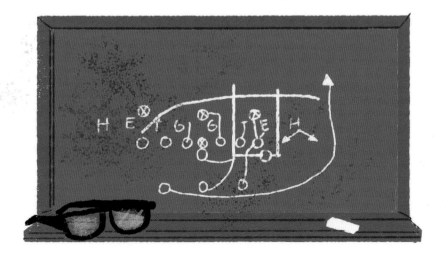

I would never forget that:

"DO BETTER TODAY THAN YOU DID YESTERDAY."

Woody talked with me a lot that day. He didn't have to, but he did.

Woody told me that he's always learning because there is always something new you can figure out.

That's why his favorite thing to do is read books. He told me that his favorite books were written by some guy named Emerson. This Emerson guy taught him how he always had to "Pay it Forward."

"Pay it Forward?" I asked.

Woody taught me that "Paying it Forward" meant when people share their wisdom or do thoughtful things for you, you Pay it Forward by sharing what you learn or by doing thoughtful things for others.

"You mean when my mom and dad tell me that they love me, I have to tell my sister that I love her?" I asked. I couldn't figure out why that was so important to Woody.

Woody finally told me that no matter what was given to me or shared with me, it didn't mean anything until I was able to "Pay it Forward" and share what I have with others.

I would never forget what he said: **"PAY IT FORWARD."**

While my friends finished up the clinic, Woody stayed with me and shared so much with me that day. I guess *he* was **"PAYING IT FORWARD."**

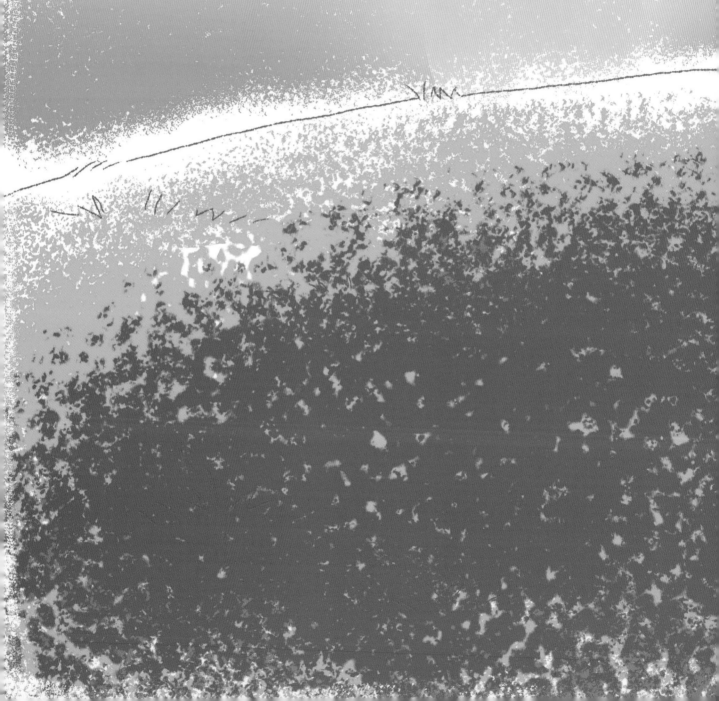

Pay it Forward

WORK HARD

DO YOUR CHORES BEFORE YOU ARE ASKED

Every Day

You can't pay back, you only pay forward

BE THOUGHTFUL

BE THANKFUL FOR YOUR GIFTS

About the Author

Roy C. Roychoudhury is a 1994 graduate of the Honors Accounting Program at The Ohio State University. Roy grew up in Marysville, Ohio, loving the Buckeyes. Whether it was counting down the months, days, minutes, then seconds to the Michigan game, or sitting on the edge of his seat listening to the Buckeyes on the radio with his brother, Roy has always had a strong passion for sports, and particularly the Buckeyes. The idea for these books germinated when Roy's youngest daughter, Maeve Anne Parker, was born. Roy's new mission was to put his older daughter, Emerson, who was two at the time, to bed each night. Emerson started to ask Roy to tell her stories, and Roy shared the tales and legends that he knew best. Emerson was riveted with each one. Some of her favorites included the 1979 Ohio State - Michigan game (now *The Buckeye Block Party*), the 1985 Ohio State - Iowa game, the 1986 Masters, and Game 6 of the 1975 World Series. Roy's wife finally suggested that other fans would probably be interested in these stories as well, so they contacted a publisher and started this journey. These are his first children's books. Roy has always had an uncanny memory for remembering minute details and facts about a multitude of games and statistics. He flexed these muscles when he won his only game show appearance on *Sports Geniuses* which aired on Fox Sports in 1999. Roy lives in Ashburn, Virginia with his wife, Anya, daughters, Emerson and Maeve Anne Parker, and dalmatians, Jaysi Mae and Sally. Roy thrives on running. He starts nearly every day with a five-mile jog. Starting in 2005, his dogs were his daily running buddies. Four years later, his daughters joined in the fun. In the true spirit of Woody Hayes, neither snow, nor rain, nor heat, nor fog, will stop him from completing his daily ritual.

For more information, please visit me at
www.buckeyekidsbooks.com